W9-AWU-709

Dear Reader,

Home, family, community and love. These are the values we cherish most in our lives—the ideals that ground us, comfort us, move us. They certainly provide the perfect inspiration around which to build a romance collection that will touch the heart.

And so we are thrilled to offer you the Harlequin Heartwarming series. Each of these special stories is a wholesome, heartfelt romance imbued with the traditional values so important to you. They are books you can share proudly with friends and family. And the authors featured in this collection are some of the most talented storytellers writing today, including favorites such as Janice Kay Johnson, Margaret Daley and Shelley Galloway. We've selected these stories especially for you based on their overriding qualities of emotion and tenderness, and they center around your favorite themes—children, weddings, second chances, the reunion of families, the quest to find a true home and, of course, sweet romance.

So curl up in your favorite chair, relax and prepare for a heartwarming reading experience!

Sincerely,

The Editors

CAROL STEWARD

To Carol Steward, selling a book is much like riding a roller coaster—every step of the process, every sale brings that exhilarating high. During the less exciting times, she's busy gathering ideas and refilling her cup. Writing brings a much-needed balance to her life, as she has her characters share lessons she herself has learned.

When she's not working at the University of Northern Colorado, you can usually find her spending time with her husband of more than thirty years, writing and being thankful she survived raising her own three children to reap the rewards of playing with her adorable grandchildren. Throughout all the different seasons of life, she's learned to simplify her life and appreciate her many blessings.

HARLEQUIN HEARTWARMING

Carol Steward

Alex's Choice

HARLEQUIN®
entertain, enrich, inspire™

Recycling programs
for this product may
not exist in your area.

ISBN-13: 978-0-373-36609-5

ALEX'S CHOICE

Copyright © 2013 by Carol Steward

Originally published as COURTING KATARINA
Copyright © 2001 by Carol Steward

www.Harlequin.com

Printed in U.S.A.

THE GOLDEN BOWL

Henry James

TOR®
A TOM DOHERTY ASSOCIATES BOOK
NEW YORK

This is a work of fiction. All the characters and events portrayed in this book are either products of the author's imagination or are used fictitiously.

THE GOLDEN BOWL

A Tor Book
Published by Tom Doherty Associates, LLC
175 Fifth Avenue
New York, NY 10010

www.tor.com

Tor® is a registered trademark of Tom Doherty Associates, LLC.

ISBN: 0-812-56510-X

First Tor edition: November 2000

Printed in the United States of America

0 9 8 7 6 5 4 3 2 1

THE GOLDEN BOWL

VOLUME ONE

THE PRINCE

1

THE PRINCE HAD ALWAYS LIKED HIS LONDON, WHEN IT had come to him; he was one of the Modern Romans who find by the Thames a more convincing image of the truth of the ancient state than any they have left by the Tiber. Brought up on the legend of the City to which the world paid tribute, he recognised in the present London much more than in contemporary Rome the real dimensions of such a case. If it was a question of an *Imperium*, he said to himself, and if one wished, as a Roman, to recover a little the sense of that, the place to do so was on London Bridge, or even, on a fine afternoon in May, at Hyde Park Corner. It was not indeed to either of those places that these grounds of his predilection, after all sufficiently vague, had, at the moment we are concerned with him, guided his steps; he had strayed simply enough into Bond Street, where his imagination, working at comparatively short range, caused him now and then to stop before a window in which objects massive and

lumpish, in silver and gold, in the forms to which precious stones contribute, or in leather, steel, brass, applied to a hundred uses and abuses, were as tumbled together as if, in the insolence of the Empire, they had been the loot of far-off victories. The young man's movements, however, betrayed no consistency of attention—not even, for that matter, when one of his arrests had proceeded from possibilities in faces shaded, as they passed him on the pavement, by huge beribboned hats, or more delicately tinted still under the tense silk of parasols held at perverse angles in waiting victorias. And the Prince's undirected thought was not a little symptomatic, since, though the turn of the season had come and the flush of the streets begun to fade, the possibilities of faces, on the August afternoon, were still one of the notes of the scene. He was too restless—that was the fact—for any concentration, and the last idea that would just now have occurred to him in any connexion was the idea of pursuit.

He had been pursuing for six months as never in his life before, and what had actually unsteadied him, as we join him, was the sense of how he had been justified. Capture had crowned the pursuit—or success, as he would otherwise have put it, had rewarded virtue; whereby the consciousness of these things made him for the hour rather serious than gay. A sobriety that might have consorted with failure sat in his handsome face, constructively regular and grave, yet at the same time oddly and, as might be, functionally almost radiant, with its dark blue eyes, its dark brown moustache and its expression no more sharply 'foreign' to an English view than to have caused it sometimes to be observed of him with a shallow felicity that he looked like a 'refined' Irishman. What had happened was that shortly before, at three o'clock, his fate had practically been sealed, and that even when one pretended to no quarrel with it the moment had something of the grimness of a crunched key in the strongest lock that could be made. There was nothing to

do as yet, further, but feel what one *had* done, and our personage felt it while he aimlessly wandered. It was already as if he were married, so definitely had the solicitors, at three o'clock, enabled the date to be fixed, and by so few days was that date now distant. He was to dine at half-past eight o'clock with the young lady on whose behalf, and on whose father's, the London lawyers had reached an inspired harmony with his own man of business, poor Calderoni, fresh from Rome and now apparently in the wondrous situation of being 'shown London', before promptly leaving it again, by Mr Verver himself, Mr Verver whose easy way with his millions had taxed to such small purpose, in the arrangements, the principle of reciprocity. The reciprocity with which the Prince was during these minutes most struck was that of Calderoni's bestowal of his company for a view of the lions. If there was one thing in the world the young man at this juncture clearly intended it was to be much more decent as a son-in-law than lots of fellows he could think of had shown themselves in that character. He thought of these fellows, from whom he was so to differ, in English; he used, mentally, the English term to describe his difference, for, familiar with the tongue from his earliest years, so that no note of strangeness remained with him either for lip or for ear, he found it convenient, in life, for the greatest number of relations. He found it convenient, oddly, even for his relation with himself—though not unmindful that there might still, as time went on, be others, including a more intimate degree of *that* one, that would seek, possibly with violence, the larger or the finer issue—which was it?—of the vernacular. Miss Verver had told him he spoke English too well—it was his only fault, and he hadn't been able to speak worse even to oblige her. 'When I speak worse, you see, I speak French,' he had said; intimating thus that there were discriminations, doubtless of the invidious kind, for which that language was the most apt. The girl had taken this, she let him

know, as a reflexion on her own French, which she had
always so dreamed of making good, of making better; to
say nothing of his evident feeling that the idiom supposed
a cleverness she was not a person to rise to. The Prince's
answer to such remarks—genial, charming, like every answer the parties to his new arrangement had yet had from
him—was that he was practising his American in order
to converse properly, on equal terms as it were, with Mr
Verver. His prospective father-in-law had a command of
it, he said, that put him at a disadvantage in any discussion; besides which he—well, besides which he had made
to the girl the observation that positively, of all his ob-
servations yet, had most finely touched her.

'You know I think he's a *real* galantuomo—"and no
mistake". There are plenty of sham ones about. He seems
to me simply the best man I've ever seen in my life.'

'Well, my dear, why shouldn't he be?' the girl had
gaily enquired.

It was this precisely that had set the Prince to think.
The things, or many of them, that had made Mr Verver
what he was seemed practically to bring a charge of waste
against the other things that, with the other people known
to the young man, had failed of such a result. 'Why his
"form",' he had returned, 'might have made one doubt.'

'Father's form?' She hadn't seen it. 'It strikes me he
hasn't got any.'

'He hasn't got mine—he hasn't even got yours.'

'Thank you for "even"!' the girl had laughed at him.

'Oh yours, my dear, is tremendous. But your father has
his own. I've made that out. So don't doubt it. It's where
it has brought him out—that's the point.'

'It's his goodness that has brought him out,' our young
woman had, at this, objected.

'Ah darling, goodness, I think, never brought any one
out. Goodness, when it's real, precisely, rather keeps people *in*.' He had been interested in his discrimination,
which amused him. 'No, it's his *way*. It belongs to him.'

But she had wondered still. 'It's the American way. That's all.'

'Exactly—it's all. It's all I say! It fits him—so it must be good for something.'

'Do you think it would be good for *you*?' Maggie Verver had smilingly asked.

To which his reply had been just of the happiest. 'I don't feel, my dear, if you really want to know, that anything much can now either hurt me or help me. Such as I am—but you'll see for yourself. Say, however, I *am* a galantuomo-which I devoutly hope: I'm like a chicken, at best, chopped up and smothered in sauce; cooked down as a *crème de volaille*, with half the parts left out. Your father's the natural fowl running about the *basse-cour*. His feathers, his movements, his sounds—those are the parts that, with me, are left out.'

'Ah as a matter of course—since you can't eat a chicken alive!'

The Prince hadn't been annoyed at this, but had been positive. 'Well, I'm eating your father alive—which is the only way to taste him. I want to continue, and as it's when he talks American that he *is* most alive, so I must also cultivate it, to get my pleasure. He couldn't make one like him so much in any other language.'

It mattered little that the girl had continued to demur—it was the mere play of her joy. 'I think he could make you like him in Chinese.'

'It would be an unnecessary trouble. What I mean is that he's a kind of result of his inevitable tone. My liking is accordingly *for* the tone—which has made him possible.'

'Oh you'll hear enough of it,' she laughed, 'before you've done with us.'

Only this in truth had made him frown a little. 'What do you mean, please, by my having "done" with you?'

'Why found out about us all there is to find.'

He had been able to take it indeed easily as a joke.

'Ah love, I *began* with that. I know enough, I feel, never to be surprised. It's you yourselves meanwhile,' he continued, 'who really know nothing. There are two parts of me'—yes, he had been moved to go on. 'One is made up of the history, the doings, the marriages, the crimes, the follies, the boundless *bêtises* of other people—especially of their infamous waste of money that might have come to me. Those things are written—literally in rows of volumes, in libraries; are as public as they're abominable. Everybody can get at them, and you've both of you wonderfully looked them in the face. But there's another part, very much smaller doubtless, which, such as it is, represents my single self, the unknown, unimportant—unimportant save to *you*—personal quantity. About this you've found out nothing.'

'Luckily, my dear,' the girl had bravely said; 'for what then would become, please, of the promised occupation of my future?'

The young man remembered even now how extraordinarily *clear*—he couldn't call it anything else—she had looked, in her prettiness, as she had said it. He also remembered what he had been moved to reply. 'The happiest reigns, we are taught, you know, are the reigns without any history.'

'Oh I'm not afraid of history!' She had been sure of that. 'Call it the bad part, if you like—yours certainly sticks out of you. What was it else,' Maggie Verver had also said, 'that made me originally think of you? It wasn't—as I should suppose you must have seen—what you call your unknown quantity, your particular self. It was the generations behind you, the follies and the crimes, the plunder and the waste—the wicked Pope, the monster most of all, whom so many of the volumes in your family library are all about. If I've read but two or three yet, I shall give myself up but the more—as soon as I have time—to the rest. Where, therefore'—she had

put it to him again—'without your archives, annals, in-
famies, would you have been?'

He recalled what, to this, he had gravely returned. 'I
might have been in a somewhat better pecuniary situation.' But his actual situation under the head in question
positively so little mattered to them that, having by that
time lived deep into the sense of his advantage, he had
kept no impression of the girl's rejoinder. It had but
sweetened the waters in which he now floated, tinted
them as by the action of some essence, poured from a
gold-topped phial, for making one's bath aromatic. No
one before him, never—not even the infamous Pope—
had so sat up to his neck in such a bath. It showed for
that matter how little one of his race could escape after
all from history. What was it but history, and of *their*
kind very much, to have the assurance of the enjoyment
of more money than the palace-builder himself could
have dreamed of? This was the element that bore him up
and into which Maggie scattered, on occasion, her ex-
quisite colouring drops. They were of the colour—of
what on earth? of what but the extraordinary American
good faith? They were of the colour of her innocence,
and yet at the same time of her imagination, with which
their relation, his and these people's, was all suffused.
What he had further said on the occasion of which we
thus represent him as catching the echoes from his own
thought while he loitered—what he had further said came
back to him, for it had been the voice itself of his luck,
the soothing sound that was always with him. 'You
Americans are almost incredibly romantic.'

'Of course we are. That's just what makes everything
so nice for us.'

'Everything?' He had wondered.

'Well, everything that's nice at all. The world, the
beautiful world—or everything in it that *is* beautiful. I
mean we see so much.'

He had looked at her a moment—and he well knew

how she had struck him, in respect to the beautiful world, as one of the beautiful, the most beautiful things. But what he had answered was: 'You see too much—that's what may sometimes make you difficulties. When you don't, at least,' he had amended with a further thought, 'see too little.' But he had quite granted that he knew what she meant, and his warning perhaps was needless. He had seen the follies of the romantic disposition, but there seemed somehow no follies in theirs—nothing, one was obliged to recognise, but innocent pleasures, pleasures without penalties. Their enjoyment was a tribute to others without being a loss to themselves. Only the funny thing, he had respectfully submitted, was that her father, though older and wiser, and a man into the bargain, was as bad—that is as good—as herself.

'Oh he's better,' the girl had freely declared—'that is he's worse. His relation to the things he cares for—and I think it beautiful—is absolutely romantic. So is his whole life over here—it's the most romantic thing I know.'

'You mean his idea for his native place?'

'Yes—the collection, the Museum with which he wishes to endow it, and of which he thinks more, as you know, than of anything in the world. It's the work of his life and the motive of everything he does.'

The young man, in his actual mood, could have smiled again—smiled delicately, as he had then smiled at her. 'Has it been his motive in letting me have you?'

'Yes, my dear, positively—or in a manner,' she had said. 'American City isn't, by the way, his native town, for, though he's not old, it's a young thing compared with him—a younger one. He started there, he has a feeling about it, and the place has grown, as he says, like the programme of a charity performance. You're at any rate a part of his collection,' she had explained—'one of the things that can only be got over here. You're a rarity, an object of beauty, an object of price. You're not perhaps

absolutely unique, but you're so curious and eminent that there are very few others like you—you belong to a class about which everything is known. You're what they call a *morceau de musée*.'

'I see. I have the great sign of it,' he had risked—'that I cost a lot of money.'

'I haven't the least idea,' she had gravely answered, 'what you cost'—and he had quite adored for the moment her way of saying it. He had felt even for the moment vulgar. But he had made the best of that.

'Wouldn't you find out if it were a question of parting with me? My value would in that case be estimated.'

She had covered him with her charming eyes, as if his value were well before her. 'Yes, if you mean that I'd pay rather than lose you.'

And then there came again what this had made him say. 'Don't talk about *me*—it's you who are not of this age. You're a creature of a braver and finer one, and the *cinquecento*, at its most golden hour, wouldn't have been ashamed of you. It would of me, and if I didn't know some of the pieces your father has acquired I should rather fear for American City the criticism of experts. Would it at all events be your idea,' he had then just ruefully asked, 'to send me there for safety?'

'Well, we may have to come to it.'

'I'll go anywhere you want.'

'We must see first—it will be only if we have to come to it. There are things,' she had gone on, 'that father puts away—the bigger and more cumbrous of course, which he stores, has already stored in masses, here and in Paris, in Italy, in Spain, in warehouses, vaults, banks, safes, wonderful secret places. We've been like a pair of pirates—positively stage pirates, the sort who wink at each other and say "Ha-ha!" when they come to where their treasure is buried. Ours is buried pretty well everywhere—except what we like to see, what we travel with and have about us. These, the smaller pieces, are the

things we take out and arrange as we can, to make the hotels we stay at and the houses we hire a little less ugly. Of course it's a danger, and we have to keep watch. But father loves a fine piece, loves, as he says, the good of it, and it's for the company of some of his things that he's willing to run his risks. And we've had extraordinary luck'—Maggie had made that point; 'we've never lost anything yet. And the finest objects are often the smallest. Values, in lots of cases, you must know, have nothing to do with size. But there's nothing, however tiny,' she had wound up, 'that we've missed.'

'I like the class,' he had laughed for this, 'in which you place me! I shall be one of the little pieces that you unpack at the hotels, or at the worst in the hired houses, like this wonderful one, and put out with the family photographs and the new magazines. But it's something not to be so big that I have to be buried.'

'Oh,' she had returned, 'you shall not be buried, my dear, till you're dead. Unless indeed you call it burial to go to American City.'

'Before I pronounce I should like to see my tomb.' So he had had, after his fashion, the last word in their interchange, save for the result of an observation that had risen to his lips at the beginning, which he had then checked, and which now came back to him. 'Good, bad or indifferent, I hope there's one thing you believe about me.'

He had sounded solemn even to himself, but she had taken it gaily. 'Ah don't fix me down to "one"! I believe things enough about you, my dear, to have a few left if most of them even go to smash. I've taken care of *that.* I've divided my faith into watertight compartments. We must manage not to sink.'

'You do believe I'm not a hypocrite? You recognise that I don't lie nor dissemble nor deceive? Is *that* watertight?'

The question, to which he had given a certain intensity, had made her, he remembered, stare an instant, her colour

rising as if it had sounded to her still stranger than he had intended. He had perceived on the spot that any *serious* discussion of veracity, of loyalty, or rather of the want of them, practically took her unprepared, as if it were quite new to her. He had noticed it before: it was the English, the American sign that duplicity, like 'love', had to be joked about. It couldn't be 'gone into'. So the note of his enquiry was—well, to call it nothing else—premature; a mistake worth making, however, for the almost overdone drollery in which her answer instinctively sought refuge.

'Water-tight—the biggest compartment of all? Why it's the best cabin and the main deck and the engine-room and the steward's pantry! It's the ship itself—it's the whole line. It's the captain's table and all one's luggage—one's reading for the trip.' She had images, like that, that were drawn from steamers and trains, from a familiarity with 'lines', a command of 'own' cars, from an experience of continents and seas, that he was unable as yet to emulate; from vast modern machineries and facilities whose acquaintance he had still to make, but as to which it was part of the interest of his situation as it stood that he could, quite without wincing, feel his future likely to bristle with them.

It was in fact, content as he was with his engagement and charming as he thought his affianced bride, his view of *that* furniture that mainly constituted our young man's 'romance'—and to an extent that made of his inward state a contrast that he was intelligent enough to feel. He was intelligent enough to feel quite humble, to wish not to be in the least hard or voracious, not to insist on his own side of the bargain, to warn himself in short against arrogance and greed. Odd enough, of a truth, was his sense of this last danger—which may illustrate moreover his general attitude toward dangers from within. Personally, he considered, he hadn't the vices in question—and that was so much to the good. His race, on the other hand,

had had them handsomely enough, and he was somehow full of his race. Its presence in him was like the consciousness of some inexpugnable scent in which his clothes, his whole person, his hands and the hair of his head, might have been steeped as in some chemical bath; the effect was nowhere in particular, yet he constantly felt himself at the mercy of the cause. He knew his antenatal history, knew it in every detail, and it was a thing to keep causes well before him. What was his frank judgement of so much of its ugliness, he asked himself, but a part of the cultivation of humility? What was this so important step he had just taken but the desire for some new history that should, so far as possible, contradict, and even if need be flatly dishonour, the old? If what had come to him wouldn't do he must *make* something different. He perfectly recognised—always in his humility—that the material for the making had to be Mr Verver's millions. There was nothing else for him on earth to make it with; he had tried before—had had to look about and see the truth. Humble as he was, at the same time he was not so humble as if he had known himself frivolous or stupid. He had an idea—which may amuse his historian—that when you were stupid enough to be mistaken about such a matter you did know it. Therefore he wasn't mistaken—his future *might* be scientific. There was nothing in himself at all events to prevent it. He was allying himself to science, for what was science but the absence of prejudice backed by the presence of money? His life would be full of machinery, which was the antidote to superstition, which was in its turn too much the consequence, or at least the exhalation, of archives. He thought of these things—of his not being at all events futile, and of his absolute acceptance of the developments of the coming age—to redress the balance of his being so differently considered. The moments when he most winced were those at which he found himself believing that, really, futility would have been forgiven him. Even *with* it,

in that absurd view, he would have been good enough. Such was the laxity, in the Ververs, of the romantic spirit. They didn't, indeed, poor dears, know what, in that line— the line of futility—the real thing meant. *He* did—having seen it, having tried it, having taken its measure. This was a memory in fact simply to screen out—much as, just in front of him while he walked, the iron shutter of a shop, closing early to the stale summer day, rattled down at the turn of some crank. There was machinery again, just as the plate glass, all about him, was money, was power, the power of the rich peoples. Well, he was *of* them now, of the rich peoples; he was on their side—if it wasn't rather the pleasanter way of putting it that they were on his.

Something of this sort was in any case the moral and the murmur of his walk. It would have been ridiculous— such a moral from such a source—if it hadn't all somehow fitted to the gravity of the hour, that gravity the oppression of which I began by recording. Another feature was the immediate nearness of the arrival of the contingent from home. He was to meet them at Charing Cross on the morrow: his younger brother, who had married before him, but whose wife, of Hebrew race, with a portion that had gilded the pill, was not in a condition to travel; his sister and her husband, the most anglicised of Milanesi; his maternal uncle, the most shelved of diplomatists; and his Roman cousin, Don Ottavio, the most *disponsible* of ex-deputies and of relatives—a scant handful of the consanguineous who, in spite of Maggie's plea for hymeneal reserve, were to accompany him to the altar. It was no great array, yet it was apparently to be a more numerous muster than any possible to the bride herself, she having no wealth of kinship to choose from and not making it up on the other hand by loose invitations. He had been interested in the girl's attitude on the matter and had wholly deferred to it, giving him, as it did, a glimpse, distinctly pleasing, of the kind of discriminations she

would in general be governed by—which were quite such as fell in with his own taste. They hadn't natural relations, she and her father, she had explained; so they wouldn't try to supply the place by artificial, by make-believe ones, by any searching of the highways and hedges. Oh yes, they had acquaintances enough—but a marriage was an intimate thing. You asked acquaintances when you *had* your kith and kin—you asked them over and above. But you didn't ask them alone, to cover your nudity and look like what they weren't. She knew what she meant and what she liked, and he was all ready to take it from her, finding a good omen in both of the facts. He expected her, desired her, to have character; his wife *should* have it, and he wasn't afraid of her having too much. He had had in his earlier time to deal with plenty of people who had had it; notably with the three or four ecclesiastics, his great-uncle the Cardinal above all, who had taken a hand and played a part in his education: the effect of all of which had never been to upset him. He was thus fairly on the look-out for the characteristic in this most intimate, as she was to become, of his associates. He encouraged it when it appeared.

He felt therefore just at present as if his papers were in order, as if his accounts so balanced as they had never done in his life before and he might close the portfolio with a snap. It would open again doubtless of itself with the arrival of the Romans; it would even perhaps open with his dining to-night in Portland Place, where Mr Verver had pitched a tent suggesting that of Alexander furnished with the spoils of Darius. But what meanwhile marked his crisis, as I have said, was his sense of the immediate two or three hours. He paused on corners, at crossings; there kept rising for him, in waves, that consciousness, sharp as to its source while vague as to its end, which I began by speaking of—the consciousness of an appeal to do something or other, before it was too late, for himself. By any friend to whom he might have

mentioned it the appeal could have been turned to frank
derision. For what, for whom indeed but himself and the
high advantages attached, was he about to marry an extraordinarily charming girl whose 'prospects', of the solid
sort, were as guaranteed as her amiability? He wasn't to
do it assuredly all for *her*. The Prince, as happened, however, was so free to feel and yet not to formulate that
there rose before him after a little, definitely, the image
of a friend whom he had often found ironic. He withheld
the tribute of attention from passing faces only to let his
impulse accumulate. Youth and beauty made him
scarcely turn, but the image of Mrs Assingham made him
presently stop a hansom. *Her* youth, her beauty were
things more or less of the past, but to find her at home,
as he possibly might, would be 'doing' what he still had
time for, would put something of a reason into his rest-
lessness and thereby probably soothe it. To recognise the
propriety of this particular pilgrimage—she lived at a due
distance, in long Cadogan Place—was already in fact to
work it off a little. A perception of the propriety of for-
mally thanking her, and of timing the act just as he happened to be doing—this, he made out as he went, was
obviously all that had been the matter with him. It was
true that he had mistaken the mood of the moment, mis-
read it rather, superficially, as an impulse to look the
other way—the other way from where his pledges had
accumulated. Mrs Assingham exactly represented and
embodied his pledges—was in her pleasant person the
force that had set them successively in motion. She had
made his marriage, quite as truly as his papal ancestor
had made his family—though he could scarce see what
she had made it for unless because she too was perversely
romantic. He had neither bribed nor persuaded her, had
given her nothing—scarce even till now articulate thanks;
so that her profit—to think of it vulgarly—must have all
had to come from the Ververs.

Yet he was far, he could still remind himself, from

supposing that she had been grossly remunerated. He was
wholly sure she hadn't; for if there were people who took
presents and people who didn't she would be quite on
the right side and of the proud class. Only then, on the
other hand, her disinterestedness was rather awful—it im-
plied, that is, such abysses of confidence. She was ad-
mirably attached to Maggie—whose possession of such
a friend might moreover quite rank as one of her 'assets';
but the great proof of her affection had been in bringing
them, with her design, together. Meeting him during a
winter in Rome, meeting him afterwards in Paris, and
'liking' him, as she had in time frankly let him know
from the first, she had marked him for her young friend's
own and had then, unmistakeably, presented him in a
light. But the interest in Maggie—that was the point—
would have achieved but little without her interest in *him*.
On what did that sentiment, unsolicited and unrecom-
pensed, rest? What good, again—for it was much like his
question about Mr Verver—should he ever have done
her? The Prince's notion of a recompense to women—
similar in this to his notion of an appeal—was more or
less to make love to them. Now he hadn't, as he believed,
made love the least little bit to Mrs Assingham—nor did
he think she had for a moment supposed it. He liked in
these days to mark them off, the women to whom he
hadn't made love: it represented—and that was what
pleased him in it—a different stage of existence from the
time at which he liked to mark off the women to whom
he had. Neither, with all this, had Mrs Assingham herself
been either aggressive or resentful. On what occasion,
ever, had she appeared to find him wanting? These things,
the motives of such people, were obscure—a little alarm-
ingly so; they contributed to that element of the impen-
etrable which alone slightly qualified his sense of his
good fortune. He remembered to have read as a boy a
wonderful tale by Allan Poe, his prospective wife's coun-
tryman—which was a thing to show, by the way, what

imagination Americans *could* have: the story of the ship-wrecked Gordon Pym, who, drifting in a small boat further toward the North Pole—or was it the South?—than any one had ever done, found at a given moment before him a thickness of white air that was like a dazzling curtain of light, concealing as darkness conceals, yet of the colour of milk or of snow. There were moments when he felt his own boat move upon some such mystery. The state of mind of his new friends, including Mrs Assingham herself, had resemblances to a great white curtain. He had never known curtains but as purple even to blackness—but as producing where they hung a darkness intended and ominous. When they were so disposed as to shelter surprises the surprises were apt to be shocks.

Shocks, however, from these quite different depths, were not what he saw reason to apprehend; what he rather seemed to himself not yet to have measured was something that, seeking a name for it, he would have called the quantity of confidence reposed in him. He had stood still, at many a moment of the previous month, with the thought, freshly determined or renewed, of the general expectation—to define it roughly—of which he was the subject. What was singular was that it seemed not so much an expectation of anything in particular as a large bland blank assumption of merits almost beyond notation, of essential quality and value. It was as if he had been some old embossed coin, of a purity of gold no longer used, stamped with glorious arms, mediæval, wonderful, of which the 'worth' in mere modern change, sovereigns and half-crowns, would be great enough, but as to which, since there were finer ways of using it, such taking to pieces was superfluous. That was the image for the security in which it was open to him to rest; he was to constitute a possession, yet was to escape being reduced to his component parts. What would this mean but that practically he was never to be tried or tested? What would it mean but that if they didn't 'change' him they really

wouldn't know—he wouldn't know himself—how many pounds, shillings and pence he had to give? These at any rate for the present were unanswerable questions; all that *was* before him was that he was invested with attributes. He was taken seriously. Lost there in the white mist was the seriousness in *them* that made them so take him. It was even in Mrs Assingham, in spite of her having, as she had frequently shown, a more mocking spirit. All he could say as yet was that he had done nothing so far to break any charm. What should he do if he were to ask her frankly this afternoon what *was*, morally speaking, behind their veil? It would come to asking what they expected him to do. She would answer him probably: 'Oh, you know, it's what we expect you to *be*!' on which he would have no resource but to deny his knowledge. Would *that* dissipate the spell, his saying he had no idea? What idea in fact could he have? He also took himself seriously—made a point of it; but it wasn't simply a question of fancy and pretension. His own estimate he saw ways, at one time and another, of dealing with; but theirs, sooner or later, say what they might, would put him to the practical proof. As the practical proof, accordingly, would naturally be proportionate to the cluster of his attributes, one arrived at a scale that he was not, honestly, the man to calculate. Who but a billionaire could say what was fair exchange for a billion? That measure was the shrouded object, but he felt really, as his cab stopped in Cadogan Place, a little nearer the shroud. He promised himself virtually to give the latter a twitch.

2

'THEY'RE NOT GOOD DAYS, YOU KNOW,' HE HAD SAID
to Fanny Assingham after declaring himself grateful for
finding her, and then, with his cup of tea, putting her in
possession of the latest news—the documents signed an
hour ago, *de part et d'autre*, and the telegram from his
backers, who had reached Paris the morning before, and
who, pausing there a little, poor dears, seemed to think
the whole thing a tremendous lark. 'We're very simple
folk, mere country cousins compared with you,' he had
also observed, 'and Paris, for my sister and her husband,
is the end of the world. London therefore will be more
or less another planet. It has always been, as with so
many of *us*, quite their Mecca, but this is their first real
caravan; they've mainly known "old England" as a shop
for articles in india-rubber and leather, in which they've
dressed themselves as much as possible. Which all
means, however, that you'll see them, all of them,
wreathed in smiles. We must be very easy with them.

Maggie's too wonderful—her preparations are on a scale! She insists on taking in the *sposi* and my uncle. The others will come to me. I've been engaging their rooms at the hotel, and with all those solemn signatures of an hour ago that brings the case home to me.'

'Do you mean you're afraid?' his hostess had amusedly asked.

'Terribly afraid. I've now but to wait to see the monster come. They're not good days; they're neither one thing nor the other. I've really *got* nothing, yet I've everything to lose. One doesn't know what still may happen.'

The way she laughed at him was for an instant almost irritating; it came out, for his fancy, from behind the white curtain. It was a sign, that is, of her deep serenity, which worried instead of soothing him. And to be soothed, after all, to be tided over, in his mystic impatience, to be told what he could understand and believe—that was what he had come for. 'Marriage then,' said Mrs Assingham, 'is what you call the monster? I admit it's a fearful thing at the best; but, for heaven's sake, if that's what you're thinking of, don't run away from it.'

'Ah to run away from it would be to run away from *you*,' the Prince replied; 'and I've already told you often enough how I depend on you to see me through.' He so liked the way she took this, from the corner of her sofa, that he gave his sincerity—for it *was* sincerity—fuller expression. 'I'm starting on the great voyage—across the unknown sea; my ship's all rigged and appointed, the cargo's stowed away and the company complete. But what seems the matter with me is that I can't sail alone; my ship must be one of a pair, must have, in the waste of waters, a—what do you call it?—a consort. I don't ask you to stay on board with me, but I must keep your sail in sight for orientation. I don't in the least myself know, I assure you, the points of the compass. But with a lead I can perfectly follow. You *must* be my lead.'

'How can you be sure,' she asked, 'where I should take you?'

'Why from your having brought me safely thus far. I should never have got here without you. You've provided the ship itself, and if you've not quite seen me aboard you've attended me ever so kindly to the dock. Your own vessel is all conveniently in the next berth, and you can't desert me now.'

She showed him again her amusement, which struck him even as excessive, as if, to his surprise, he made her also a little nervous; she treated him in fine as if he were not uttering truths but making pretty figures for her diversion. 'My vessel, dear Prince?' she smiled. 'What vessel in the world have I? This little house is all our ship, Bob's and mine—and thankful we are now to have it. We've wandered far, living, as you may say, from hand to mouth, without rest for the soles of our feet. But the time has come for us at last to draw in.'

He made at this, the young man, an indignant protest. 'You talk about rest—it's too selfish!—when you're just launching me on adventures?'

She shook her head with her kind lucidity. 'Not adventures—heaven forbid! You've had yours—as I've had mine; and my idea has been all along that we should neither of us begin again. My own last, precisely, has been doing for you all you so prettily mention. But it consists simply in having conducted you to rest. You talk about ships, but they're not the comparison. Your tossings are over—you're practically *in* port. The port,' she concluded, 'of the Golden Isles.'

He looked about, to put himself more in relation with the place; then after an hesitation seemed to speak certain words instead of certain others. 'Oh I know where I *am*—! I do decline to be left, but what I came for of course was to thank you. If to-day has seemed for the first time the end of preliminaries, I feel how little there would have been any at all without you. The first were wholly yours.'

'Well,' said Mrs Assingham, 'they were remarkably easy. I've seen them, I've *had* them,' she smiled, 'more difficult. Everything, you must feel, went of itself. So, you must feel, everything still goes.'

The Prince quickly agreed. 'Oh beautifully! But you had the conception.'

'Ah Prince, so had you!'

He looked at her harder a moment. 'You had it first. You had it most.'

She returned his look as if it had made her wonder. 'I *liked* it, if that's what you mean. But you liked it surely yourself. I protest that I had easy work with you. I had only at last—when I thought it was time—to speak for you.'

'All that's quite true. But you're leaving me all the same, you're leaving me—you're washing your hands of me,' he went on. 'However, that won't be easy; I won't *be* left.' And he had turned his eyes about again, taking in the pretty room that she had just described as her final refuge, the place of peace for a world-worn couple, to which she had lately retired with 'Bob'. 'I shall keep this spot in sight. Say what you will I shall need you. I'm not, you know,' he declared, 'going to give you up for anybody.'

'If you're afraid—which of course you're not—are you trying to make me the same?' she asked after a moment.

He waited a minute too, then answered her with a question. 'You say you "liked" it, your undertaking to make my engagement possible. It remains beautiful for me that you did; it's charming and unforgettable. But still more it's mysterious and wonderful. *Why*, you dear delightful woman, did you like it?'

'I scarce know what to make,' she said, 'of such an enquiry. If you haven't by this time found out yourself, what meaning can anything I say have for you? Don't you really after all feel,' she added while nothing came

from him—'aren't you conscious every minute of the perfection of the creature of whom I've put you into possession?'

'Every minute—gratefully conscious. But that's exactly the ground of my question. It wasn't only a matter of your handing *me* over—it was a matter of your handing her. It was a matter of *her* fate still more than of mine. You thought all the good of her that one woman can think of another, and yet, by your account, you enjoyed assisting at her risk.'

She had kept her eyes on him while he spoke, and this was what visibly determined a repetition for her. 'Are you trying to frighten me?'

'Ah that's a foolish view—I should be too vulgar. You apparently can't understand either my good faith or my humility. I'm awfully humble,' the young man insisted; 'that's the way I've been feeling to-day, with everything so finished and ready. And you won't take me for serious.'

She continued to face him as if he really troubled her a little. 'Oh you deep old Italians!'

'There you are,' he returned—'it's what I wanted you to come to. That's the responsible note.'

'Yes,' she went on—'if you're "humble" you must be dangerous.' She had a pause while he only smiled; then she said: 'I don't in the least want to lose sight of you. But even if I did I shouldn't think it right.'

'Thank you for that—it's what I needed of you. I'm sure, after all, that the more you're with me the more I shall understand. It's the only thing in the world I want. I'm excellent, I really think, all round—except that I'm stupid. I can do pretty well anything I see. But I've got to see it first.' And he pursued his demonstration. 'I don't in the least mind its having to be shown me—in fact I like that better. Therefore it is that I want, that I shall always want, your eyes. Through them I wish to look—even at any risk of their showing me what I mayn't like.

For then,' he wound up, 'I shall know. And of that I shall never be afraid.'

She might quite have been waiting to see what he would come to, but she spoke with a certain impatience. 'What on earth are you talking about?'

But he could perfectly say: 'Of my real honest fear of being "off" some day, of being wrong, *without* knowing it. That's what I shall always trust you for—to tell me when I am. No—with you people it's a sense. We haven't got it—not as you have. Therefore—!' But he had said enough. 'Ecco!' he simply smiled.

It was not to be concealed that he worked upon her, but of course she had always liked him. 'I should be interested,' she presently remarked, 'to see some sense *you* don't possess.'

Well, he produced one on the spot. 'The moral, dear Mrs Assingham. I mean always as you others consider it. I've of course something that in our poor dear backward old Rome sufficiently passes for it. But it's no more like yours than the tortuous stone staircase—half-ruined into the bargain!—in some castle of our *quattrocento* is like the "lightning elevator" in one of Mr Verver's fifteen-storey buildings. Your moral sense works by steam—it sends you up like a rocket. Ours is slow and steep and unlighted, with so many of the steps missing that—well, that it's as short in almost any case to turn round and come down again.'

'Trusting,' Mrs Assingham smiled, 'to get up some other way?'

'Yes—or not to have to get up at all. However,' he added, 'I told you that at the beginning.'

'Machiavelli!' she simply exclaimed.

'You do me too much honour. I wish indeed I had his genius. However, if you really believed I have his perversity you wouldn't say it. But it's all right,' he gaily enough concluded; 'I shall always have you to come to.'

On this, for a little, they sat face to face; after which,

without comment, she asked him if he would have more
tea. All she would give him, he promptly signified; and
he developed, making her laugh, his idea that the tea of
the English race was somehow their morality, 'made',
with boiling water, in a little pot, so that the more of it
one drank the more moral one would become. His drollery served as a transition, and she put to him several
questions about his sister and the others, questions as to
what Bob, in particular, Colonel Assingham, her husband,
could do for the arriving gentlemen, whom, by the
Prince's leave, he would immediately go to see. He was
funny, while they talked, about his own people too,
whom he described, with anecdotes of their habits, imi-
tations of their manners and prophecies of their conduct,
as more *rococo* than anything Cadogan Place would ever
have known. This, Mrs Assingham professed, was exactly
what would endear them to her, and that in turn drew
from her visitor a fresh declaration of all the comfort of
his being able so to depend on her. He had been with her
at this point some twenty minutes; but he had paid her
much longer visits, and he stayed now as if to make his
attitude prove his appreciation. He stayed moreover—*that*
was really the sign of the hour—in spite of the nervous
unrest that had brought him and that had in truth much
rather fed on the scepticism by which she had apparently
meant to soothe it. She hadn't soothed him, and there
arrived remarkably a moment when the cause of her failure gleamed out. He hadn't frightened her, as she called
it—he felt that; yet she was herself not at ease. She had
been nervous, though trying to disguise it; the sight of
him, following on the announcement of his name, had
shown her as disconcerted. This conviction, for the young
man, deepened and sharpened; yet with the effect too of
making him glad in spite of it. It was as if, in calling, he
had done even better than he intended. For it was somehow *important*—that was what it was—that there should
be at this hour something the matter with Mrs Assingham,

with whom, in all their acquaintance, so considerable now, there had never been the least little thing the matter. To wait thus and watch for it was to know of a truth that there was something the matter with *him*; since—strangely, with so little to go upon—his heart had positively begun to beat to the time of suspense. It fairly befell at last for a climax that they almost ceased to pretend—to pretend, that is, to cheat each other with forms. The unspoken had come up, and there was a crisis—neither could have said how long it lasted—during which they were reduced, for all interchange, to looking at each other on quite an inordinate scale. They might at this moment, in their positively portentous stillness, have been keeping it up for a wager, sitting for their photograph or even enacting a *tableau-vivant*.

The spectator of whom they would thus well have been worthy might have read meanings of his own into the intensity of their communion—or indeed, even without meanings, have found his account, æsthetically, in some gratified play of our modern sense of type, so scantly to be distinguished from our modern sense of beauty. Type was there, at the worst, in Mrs Assingham's dark neat head, on which the crisp black hair made waves so fine and so numerous that she looked even more in the fashion of the hour than she desired. Full of discriminations against the obvious, she had yet to accept a flagrant appearance and to make the best of misleading signs. Her richness of hue, her generous nose, her eyebrows marked like those of an actress—these things, with an added amplitude of person on which middle age had set its seal, seemed to present her insistently as a daughter of the South, or still more of the East, a creature formed by hammocks and divans, fed upon sherbets and waited upon by slaves. She looked as if her most active effort might be to take up, as she lay back, her mandolin, or to share a sugared fruit with a pet gazelle. She was in fact however neither a pampered Jewess nor a lazy Creole;

New York had been recordedly her birthplace and 'Europe' punctually her discipline. She wore yellow and purple because she thought it better, as she said, while one was about it, to look like the Queen of Sheba than like a *revendeuse*; she put pearls in her hair and crimson and gold in her tea-gown for the same reason: it was her theory that nature itself had overdressed her and that her only course was to drown, as it was hopeless to try to chasten, the over-dressing. So she was covered and surrounded with 'things', which were frankly toys and shams, a part of the amusement with which she rejoiced to supply her friends. These friends were in the game—that of playing with the disparity between her aspect and her character. Her character was attested by the second movement of her face, which convinced the beholder that her vision of the humours of the world was not supine, not passive. She enjoyed, she needed the warm air of friendship, but the eyes of the American city looked out, somehow, for the opportunity of it, from under the lids of Jerusalem. With her false indolence, in short, her false leisure, her false pearls and palms and courts and fountains, she was a person for whom life was multitudinous detail, detail that left her, as it at any moment found her, unappalled and unwearied.

'Sophisticated as I may appear'—it was her frequent phrase—she had found sympathy her best resource. It gave her plenty to do; it made her, as she also said, sit up. She had in her life two great holes to fill, and she described herself as dropping social scraps into them as she had known old ladies, in her early American time, drop morsels of silk into the baskets in which they collected the material for some eventual patchwork quilt. One of these gaps in Mrs Assingham's completeness was her want of children; the other was her want of wealth. It was wonderful how little either, in the fulness of time, came to show; sympathy and curiosity could render their objects practically filial, just as an English husband who

in his military years had 'run' everything in his regiment
could make economy blossom like the rose. Colonel Bob
had, a few years after his marriage, left the army, which
had clearly by that time done its laudable all for the en-
richment of his personal experience, and he could thus
give his whole time to the gardening in question. There
reigned among the younger friends of this couple a legend, almost too venerable for historical criticism, that the
marriage itself, the happiest of its class, dated from the
far twilight of the age, a primitive period when such
things—such things as American girls accepted as 'good
enough'—hadn't begun to be; so that the pleasant pair
had been, as to the risk taken on either side, bold and
original, honourably marked, for the evening of life, as
discoverers of a kind of hymeneal Northwest Passage.
Mrs Assingham knew better, knew there had been no
historic hour, from that of Pocahontas down, when some
young Englishman hadn't precipitately believed and some
American girl hadn't, with a few more gradations, availed
herself to the full of her incapacity to doubt; but she accepted resignedly the laurel of the founder, since she was
in fact pretty well the *doyenne*, above ground, of her
transplanted tribe, and since, above all, she *had* invented
combinations, though she hadn't invented Bob's own. It
was he who had done that, absolutely puzzled it out by
himself from its first odd glimmer—resting upon it moreover, through the years to come, as proof enough in him
by itself of the higher cleverness. If she kept her own
cleverness up it was largely that he should have full
credit. There were moments in truth when she privately
felt how little—striking out as he had done—he could
have afforded that she should show the common limits.
But Mrs Assingham's cleverness was in truth tested when
her present visitor at last said to her: 'I don't think, you
know; that you're treating me quite right. You've something on your mind that you don't tell me.'

It was positive too that her smile of reply was a trifle

dim. 'Am I obliged to tell you everything I have on my mind?'

'It isn't a question of everything, but it's a question of anything that may particularly concern me. Then you shouldn't keep it back. You know with what care I desire to proceed, taking everything into account and making no mistake that may possibly injure *her*.'

Mrs Assingham, at this, had after an instant an odd interrogation. ' "Her"?'

'Her and him. Both our friends. Either Maggie or her father.'

'I *have* something on my mind,' Mrs Assingham presently returned; 'something has happened for which I hadn't been prepared. But it isn't anything that properly concerns you.'

The Prince, with immediate gaiety, threw back his head. 'What do you mean by "properly"? I somehow see volumes in it. It's the way people put a thing when they put it—well, wrong. *I* put things right. What is it that has happened for me?'

His hostess had the next moment drawn spirit from his tone. 'Oh I shall be delighted if you'll take your share of it. Charlotte Stant's in London. She has just been here.'

'Miss Stant? Oh really?' The Prince expressed clear surprise—a transparency through which his eyes met his friend's with a certain hardness of concussion. 'She has arrived from America?' he then quickly asked.

'She appears to have arrived this noon—coming up from Southampton—at an hotel. She dropped upon me after luncheon and was here for more than an hour.'

The young man heard with interest, though not with an interest too great for his gaiety. 'You think then I've a share in it? What *is* my share?'

'Why any you like—the one you seemed just now eager to take. It was you yourself who insisted.'

He looked at her on this with conscious inconsistency, and she could now see that he had changed colour. But

he was always easy. 'I didn't know then what the matter was.'

'You didn't think it could be so bad?'

'Do you call it very bad?' the young man asked.

'Only,' she smiled, 'because that's the way it seems to affect *you*.'

He hesitated, still with the trace of his quickened colour, still looking at her, still adjusting his manner. 'But you allowed you were upset.'

'To the extent—yes—of not having in the least looked for her. Any more,' said Mrs Assingham, 'than I judge Maggie to have done.'

The Prince thought; then as if glad to be able to say something very natural and true: 'No—quite right. Maggie hasn't looked for her. But I'm sure,' he added, 'she'll be delighted to see her.'

'*That* certainly'—and his hostess spoke with a different shade of gravity.

'She'll be quite overjoyed,' the Prince went on. 'Has Miss Stant now gone to her?'

'She has gone back to her hotel, to bring her things here. I can't have her,' said Mrs Assingham, 'alone at an hotel.'

'No; I see.'

'If she's here at all she must stay with me.'

He quite took it in. 'So she's coming now?'

'I expect her at any moment. If you wait you'll see her.'

'Oh,' he promptly declared—'charming!' But this word came out as if a little in sudden substitution for some other. It sounded accidental, whereas he wished to be firm. That accordingly was what he next showed himself. 'If it wasn't for what's going on these next days Maggie would certainly want to have her. In fact,' he lucidly continued, 'isn't what's happening just a reason to *make* her want to?' Mrs Assingham, for answer, only looked at him, and this the next instant had apparently

had more effect than if she had spoken. For he asked a question that seemed incongruous. 'What has she come *for*?'

It made his companion laugh. 'Why, for just what you say. For your marriage.'

'Mine?'—He wondered.

'Maggie's—it's the same thing. It's "for" your great event. And then,' said Mrs Assingham, 'she's so lonely.'

'Has she given you that as a reason?'

'I scarcely remember—she gave me so many. She abounds, poor dear, in reasons. But there's one that, whatever she does, I always remember for myself.'

'And which is that?' He looked as if he ought to guess but couldn't.

'Why the fact that she has no home—absolutely none whatever. She's extraordinarily alone.'

Again he took it in. 'And also has no great means.'

'Very small ones. Which is not however, with the expense of railways and hotels, a reason for her running to and fro.'

'On the contrary. But she doesn't like her country.'

'Hers, my dear man?—it's little enough "hers".' The attribution for the moment amused his hostess. 'She has rebounded now—but she has had little enough else to do with it.'

'Oh I say hers,' the Prince pleasantly explained, 'very much as at this time of day I might say mine. I quite feel, I assure you, as if the great place already more or less belonged to *me*.'

'That's your good fortune and your point of view. You own—or you soon practically *will* own—so much of it. Charlotte owns almost nothing in the world, she tells me, but two colossal trunks—only one of which I've given her leave to introduce into this house. She'll depreciate to you,' Mrs Assingham added, 'your property.'

He thought of these things, he thought of everything; but he had always his resource at hand of turning all to

the easy. 'Has she come with designs upon me?' And then in a moment, as if even this were almost too grave, he sounded the note that had least to do with himself. 'Est-elle toujours aussi belle?' That was the furthest point, somehow, to which Charlotte Stant could be relegated.

Mrs Assingham treated it freely. 'Just the same. The person in the world, to my sense, whose looks are most subject to appreciation. It's all in the way she affects you. One admires her if one doesn't happen not to. So, as well, one criticises her.'

'Ah that's not fair!' said the Prince.

'To criticise her? Then there you are! You're answered.'

'I'm answered.' He took it, humorously, as his lesson—sank his previous self-consciousness, with excellent effect, in grateful docility. 'I only meant that there are perhaps better things to be done with Miss Stant than to criticise her. When once you begin *that*, with any one—!' He was vague and kind.

'I quite agree that it's better to keep out of it as long as one can. But when one *must* do it—'

'Yes?' he asked as she paused.

'Then know what you mean.'

'I see. Perhaps,' he smiled, '*I* don't know what I mean.'

'Well, it's what, just now, in all ways, you particularly should know.' Mrs Assingham however made no more of this, having before anything else apparently a scruple about the tone she had just used. 'I quite understand of course that, given her great friendship with Maggie, she should have wanted to be present. She has acted impulsively—but she has acted generously.'

'She has acted beautifully,' said the Prince.

'I say "generously" because I mean she hasn't in any way counted the cost. She'll have it to count in a manner now,' his hostess continued. 'But that doesn't matter.'

He could see how little. 'You'll look after her.'

'I'll look after her.'

'So it's all right.'

'It's all right,' said Mrs Assingham.

'Then why are you troubled?'

It pulled her up—but only for a minute. 'I'm not—any more than you.'

The Prince's dark blue eyes were of the finest and, on occasion, precisely, resembled nothing so much as the high windows of a Roman palace, of an historic front by one of the great old designers, thrown open on a feast-day to the golden air. His look itself at such times suggested an image—that of some very noble personage who, expected, acclaimed by the crowd in the street and with old precious stuffs falling over the sill for his support, had gaily and gallantly come to show himself: always moreover less in his own interest than in that of spectators and subjects whose need to admire, even to gape, was periodically to be considered. The young man's expression became after this fashion something vivid and concrete—a beautiful personal presence, that of a prince in very truth, a ruler, warrior, patron, lighting up brave architecture and diffusing the sense of a function. It had been happily said of his face that the figure thus appearing in the great frame was the ghost of some proudest ancestor. Whoever the ancestor now, at all events, the Prince was, for Mrs Assingham's benefit, in view of the people. He seemed, leaning on crimson damask, to take in the bright day. He looked younger than his years; he was beautiful innocent vague. 'Oh well, *I'm* not!' he rang out clear.

'I should like to *see* you, sir!' she said. 'For you wouldn't have a shadow of excuse.' He showed how he agreed that he would have been at a loss for one, and the fact of their serenity was thus made as important as if some danger of its opposite had directly menaced them. The only thing was that if the evidence of their cheer was

so established Mrs Assingham had a little to explain her original manner, and she came to this before they dropped the question. 'My first impulse is always to behave about everything as if I feared complications. But I don't fear them—I really like them. They're quite my element.'

He deferred for her to this account of herself. 'But still,' he said, 'if we're not in the presence of a complication.'

She debated. 'A handsome clever odd girl staying with one is always a complication.'

The young man weighed it almost as if the question were new to him. 'And will she stay very long?'

His friend gave a laugh. 'How in the world can I know? I've scarcely asked her.'

'Ah yes. You can't.'

But something in the tone of it amused her afresh. 'Do you think *you* could?'

'I?' He wondered.

'Do you think you could get it out of her for me—the probable length of her stay?'

He rose bravely enough to the occasion and the challenge. 'I dare say if you were to give me the chance.'

'Here it is then for you,' she answered; for she had heard, within the minute, the stop of a cab at her door. 'She's back.'

3

IT HAD BEEN SAID AS A JOKE, BUT AS AFTER THIS THEY awaited their friend in silence the effect of the silence was to turn the time to gravity—a gravity not dissipated even when the Prince next spoke. He had been thinking the case over and making up his mind. A handsome clever odd girl staying with one *was* a complication. Mrs Assingham so far was right. But there were the facts— the good relations, from schooldays, of the two young women, and the clear confidence with which one of them had arrived. 'She can come, you know, at any time, to *us*.'

Mrs Assingham took it up with an irony beyond laughter. 'You'd like her for your honeymoon?'

'Oh no, you must keep her for that. But why not after?'

She had looked at him a minute; then at the sound of a voice in the corridor they had got up. 'Why not? You're splendid!'

Charlotte Stant, the next minute, was with them, ush-

ered in as she had alighted from her cab and prepared for not finding Mrs Assingham alone—this would have been to be noticed—by the butler's answer, on the stairs, to a question put to him. She could have looked at that lady with such straightness and brightness only from knowing that the Prince was also there—the discrimination of but a moment, yet which let him take her in still better than if she had instantly faced him. He availed himself of the chance thus given him, for he was conscious of all these things. What he accordingly saw for some seconds with intensity was a tall strong charming girl who wore for him at first exactly the air of her adventurous situation, a reference in all her person, in motion and gesture, in free vivid yet altogether happy indications of dress, from the becoming compactness of her hat to the shade of tan in her shoes, to winds and waves and custom-houses, to far countries and long journeys, the knowledge of how and where and the habit, founded on experience, of not being afraid. He was aware at the same time that of this combination the 'strong-minded' note was not, as might have been apprehended, the basis; he was now sufficiently familiar with English-speaking types, he had sounded attentively enough such possibilities, for a quick vision of differences. He had besides his own view of this young lady's strength of mind. It was great, he had ground to believe, but it would never interfere with the play of her extremely personal, her always amusing taste. This last was the thing in her—for she threw it out positively on the spot like a light—that she might have reappeared, during these moments, just to cool his worried eyes with. He saw her in her light: that immediate exclusive address to their friend was like a lamp she was holding aloft for his benefit and for his pleasure. It showed him everything—above all her presence in the world, so closely, so irretrievably contemporaneous with his own: a sharp, sharp fact, sharper during these instants than any other at all, even than that of his marriage, but accompanied, in

a subordinate and controlled way, with those others, facial, physiognomic, that Mrs Assingham had been speaking of as subject to appreciation. So they were, these others, as he met them again, and that was the connexion they instantly established with him. If they had to be interpreted this made at least for intimacy. There was but one way certainly for *him*—to interpret them in the sense of the already known.

Making use then of clumsy terms of excess, the face was too narrow and too long, the eyes not large, and the mouth on the other hand by no means small, with substance in its lips and a slight, the very slightest, tendency to protrusion in the solid teeth, otherwise indeed well arrayed and flashingly white. But it was, strangely, as a cluster of possessions of his own that these things in Charlotte Stant now affected him; items in a full list, items recognised, each of them, as if, for the long interval, they had been 'stored'—wrapped up, numbered, put away in a cabinet. While she faced Mrs Assingham the door of the cabinet had opened of itself; he took the relics out one by one, and it was more and more each instant as if she were giving him time. He saw again that her thick hair was, vulgarly speaking, brown, but that there was a shade of tawny autumn leaf in it for 'appreciation'—a colour indescribable and of which he had known no other case, something that gave her at moments the sylvan head of a huntress. He saw the sleeves of her jacket drawn to her wrists, but he again made out the free arms within them to be of the completely rounded, the polished slimness that Florentine sculptors in the great time had loved and of which the apparent firmness is expressed in their old silver and old bronze. He knew her narrow hands, he knew her long fingers and the shape and colour of her finger-nails, he knew her special beauty of movement and line when she turned her back, and the perfect working of all her main attachments, that of some wonderful finished instrument, something intently made

for exhibition, for a prize. He knew above all the extraordinary fineness of her flexible waist, the stem of an expanded flower, which gave her a likeness also to some long loose silk purse, well filled with gold-pieces, but having been passed empty through a finger-ring that held it together. It was as if, before she turned to him, he had weighed the whole thing in his open palm and even heard a little the chink of the metal. When she did turn to him it was to recognise with her eyes what he might have been doing. She made no circumstance of thus coming upon him, save so far as the intelligence in her face could at any moment make a circumstance of almost anything. If when she moved off she looked like a huntress, she looked when she came nearer like his notion, perhaps not wholly correct, of a muse. But what she said was simply: 'You see you're not rid of me. How is dear Maggie?'

It was to come soon enough by the quite unforced operation of chance, the young man's opportunity to ask her the question suggested by Mrs Assingham shortly before her entrance. The licence, had he chosen to embrace it, was within a few minutes all there—the licence given him literally to enquire of this young lady how long she was likely to be with them. For a matter of the mere domestic order had quickly determined on Mrs Assingham's part a withdrawal, of a few moments, which had the effect of leaving her visitors free. 'Mrs Betterman's there?' she had said to Charlotte in allusion to some member of the household who was to have received her and seen her belongings settled; to which Charlotte had replied that she had encountered only the butler, who had been quite charming. She had deprecated any action taken on behalf of her effects; but her hostess, rebounding from accumulated cushions, evidently saw more in Mrs Betterman's non-appearance than could meet the casual eye. What she saw in short demanded her intervention, in spite of an earnest 'Let *me* go!' from the girl, and a prolonged smiling wail over the trouble she was giving.

The Prince was quite aware at this moment that departure, for himself, was indicated; the question of Miss Stant's installation didn't demand his presence; it was a case for one to go away—if one hadn't a reason for staying. He had a reason, however—of that he was equally aware; and he hadn't for a good while done anything more conscious and intentional than not quickly to take leave. His visible insistence—for it came to that—even demanded of him a certain disagreeable effort, the sort of effort he had mostly associated with acting for an idea. His idea was there, his idea was to find out something, something he wanted much to know, and to find it out not tomorrow, not at some future time, not in short with waiting and wondering, but if possible before quitting the place. This particular curiosity moreover confounded itself a little with the occasion offered him to satisfy Mrs Assingham's own; he wouldn't have admitted that he was staying to ask a rude question—there was distinctly nothing rude in his having his reasons. It would be rude for that matter to turn one's back without a word or two on an old friend.

Well, as it came to pass, he got the word or two, for Mrs Assingham's preoccupation was practically simplifying. The little crisis was of shorter duration than our account of it; duration would naturally have forced him to take up his hat. He was somehow glad, on finding himself alone with Charlotte, that he hadn't been guilty of that inconsequence. Not to be flurried was the kind of consistency he wanted, just as consistency was the kind of dignity. And why couldn't he have dignity when he had so much of the good conscience, as it were, on which such advantages rested? He had done nothing he oughtn't—he had in fact done nothing at all. Once more, as a man conscious of having known many women, he could assist, as he would have called it, at the recurrent, the predestined phenomenon, the thing always as certain as sunrise or the coming round of saints' days, the doing

by the woman of the thing that gave her away. She did it, ever, inevitably, infallibly—she couldn't possibly not do it. It was her nature, it was her life, and the man could always expect it without lifting a finger. This was *his*, the man's, any man's, position and strength—that he had necessarily the advantage, that he only had to wait with a decent patience to be placed, in spite of himself, it might really be said, in the right. Just so the punctuality of performance on the part of the other creature was her weakness and her deep misfortune—not less, no doubt, than her beauty. It produced for the man that extraordinary mixture of pity and profit in which his relation with her, when he was not a mere brute, mainly consisted; and gave him in fact his most pertinent ground of being always nice to her, nice about her, nice *for* her. She always dressed her act up, of course, she muffled and disguised and arranged it, showing in fact in these dissimulations a cleverness equal to but one thing in the world, equal to her abjection: she would let it be known for anything, for everything, but the truth of which it was made. That was what, exactly, Charlotte Stant would be doing now; that was the present motive and support, to a certainty, of each of her looks and motions. She was the twentieth woman, she was possessed by her doom, but her doom was also to arrange appearances, and what now concerned him was to learn how she proposed. He would help her, would arrange *with* her—to any point in reason; the only thing was to know what appearance could best be produced and best be preserved. Produced and preserved on her part of course; since on his own there had been luckily no folly to cover up, nothing but a perfect accord between conduct and obligation.

They stood there together at all events, when the door had closed behind their friend, with a conscious strained smile and very much as if each waited for the other to strike the note or give the pitch. The young man held himself, in his silent suspense—only not more afraid be-

cause he felt her own fear. She was afraid of herself,
however; whereas, to his gain of lucidity, he was afraid
only of her. Would she throw herself into his arms or
would she be otherwise wonderful? She would see what
he would do—so their queer minute without words told
him; and she would act accordingly. But what could he
do but just let her see that he would make anything,
everything, for her, as honourably easy as possible? Even
if she should throw herself into his arms he would make
that easy—easy, that is, to overlook, to ignore, not to
remember, and not by the same token either to regret.
This was not what in fact happened, though it was also
not at a single touch, but by the finest gradations, that his
tension subsided. 'It's too delightful to be back!' she said
at last; and it was all she definitely gave him—being
moreover nothing but what any one else might have said.
Yet with two or three other things that, on his response,
followed it, it quite pointed the path, while the tone of it,
and her whole attitude, were as far removed as need have
been from the truth of her situation. The abjection that
was present to him as of the essence quite failed to peep
out, and he soon enough saw that if she was arranging
she could be trusted to arrange. Good—it was all he
asked; and all the more that he could admire and like her
for it. The particular appearance she would, as they said,
go in for was that of having no account whatever to give
him—it would be in fact that of having none to give
anybody—of reasons or of motives, of comings or of
goings. She was a charming young woman who had met
him before, but she was also a charming young woman
with a life of her own. She would take it high—up, up,
up, ever so high. Well then he would do the same; no
height would be too great for them, not even the dizziest
conceivable to a young person so subtle. The dizziest
seemed indeed attained when after another moment she
came as near as she was to come to an apology for her
abruptness.

'I've been thinking of Maggie, and at last I yearned for her. I wanted to see her happy—and it doesn't strike me I find you too shy to tell me I *shall*.'

'Of course she's happy, thank God! Only it's almost terrible, you know, the happiness of young good generous creatures. It rather frightens one. But the Blessed Virgin and all the Saints,' said the Prince, 'have her in their keeping.'

'Certainly they have. She's the dearest of the dear. But I needn't tell you,' the girl added.

'Ah,' he returned with gravity, 'I feel that I've still much to learn about her.' To which he subjoined: 'She'll rejoice awfully in your being with us.'

'Oh you don't need me!' Charlotte smiled. 'It's her hour. It's a great hour. One has seen often enough, with girls, what it is. But that,' she said, 'is exactly why. Why I've wanted, I mean, not to miss it.'

He bent on her a kind comprehending face. 'You mustn't miss anything.' He had got it, the pitch, and he could keep it now, for all he had needed was to have it given him. The pitch was the happiness of his wife that was to be—the sight of that happiness as a joy for an old friend. It was, yes, magnificent, and not the less so for its coming to him suddenly as sincere, as nobly exalted. Something in Charlotte's eyes seemed to tell him this, seemed to plead with him in advance as to what he was to find in it. He was eager—and he tried to show her that too—to find what she liked; mindful as he easily could be of what the friendship had been for Maggie. It had been armed with the wings of young imagination, young generosity; it had been, he believed—always counting out her intense devotion to her father—the liveliest emotion she had known before the dawn of the sentiment inspired by himself. She hadn't, to his knowledge, invited the object of it to their wedding, hadn't thought of proposing to her, for a matter of a couple of hours, an arduous and expensive journey. But she had kept her connected and

informed, from week to week, in spite of preparations and absorptions. 'Oh I've been writing to Charlotte—I wish you knew her better'; he could still hear, from recent weeks, this record of the fact, just as he could still be conscious, not otherwise than queerly, of the gratuitous element in Maggie's wish, which he had failed as yet to indicate to her. Older and perhaps more intelligent, at any rate, why shouldn't Charlotte respond—and be quite *free* to respond—to such fidelities with something more than mere formal good manners? The relations of women with each other were of the strangest, it was true, and he probably wouldn't have trusted here a young person of his own race. He was proceeding throughout on the ground of the immense difference—difficult indeed as it might have been to disembroil in this young person *her* race-quality. Nothing in her definitely placed her; she was a rare, a special product. Her singleness, her solitude, her want of means, that is her want of ramifications and other advantages, contributed to enrich her somehow with an odd precious neutrality, to constitute for her, so detached yet so aware, a sort of small social capital. It was the only one she had—it was the only one a lonely gregarious girl *could* have, since few surely had in anything like the same degree arrived at it, and since this one indeed had compassed it but through the play of some gift of nature to which you could scarce give a definite name.

It wasn't a question of her strange sense for tongues, with which she juggled as a conjuror at a show juggled with balls or hoops or lighted brands—it wasn't at least entirely that, for he had known people almost as polyglot whom their accomplishment had quite failed to make interesting. He was polyglot himself, for that matter—as was the case too with so many of his friends and relations; for none of whom more than for himself was it anything but a common convenience. The point was that in this young woman it was a beauty in itself, and almost a mystery: so, certainly, he had more than once felt in

noting on her lips that rarest, among the Barbarians, of all civil graces, a perfect felicity in the use of Italian. He had known strangers—a few, and mostly men—who spoke his own language agreeably; but he had known neither man nor woman who showed for it Charlotte's almost mystifying instinct. He remembered how, from the first of their acquaintance, she had made no display of it, quite as if English, between them, his English so matching with hers, were their inevitable medium. He had perceived all by accident—by hearing her talk before him to somebody else—that they had an alternative as good; an alternative in fact as much better as the amusement for him was greater in watching her for the slips that never came. Her account of the mystery didn't suffice: her recall of her birth in Florence and Florentine childhood; her parents, from the great country, but themselves already of a corrupt generation, demoralised falsified polyglot well before her, with the Tuscan balia who was her first remembrance; the servants of the villa, the dear contadini of the podere, the little girls and the other peasants of the next podere, all the rather shabby but still ever so pretty human furniture of her early time, including the good sisters of the poor convent of the Tuscan hills, the convent shabbier than almost anything else, but prettier too, in which she had been kept at school till the subsequent phase, the phase of the much grander institution in Paris at which Maggie was to arrive, terribly frightened and as a smaller girl, three years before her own ending of her period of five. Such reminiscences naturally gave a ground, but they hadn't prevented him from insisting that some strictly civil ancestor—generations back, and from the Tuscan hills if she would—made himself felt ineffaceably in her blood and in her tone. She knew nothing of the ancestor, but she had taken his theory from him, gracefully enough, as one of the little presents that make friendship flourish. These matters, however, all melted together now, though a sense of them was doubt-

less concerned, not unnaturally, in the next thing, of the nature of a surmise, that his discretion let him articulate. 'You haven't, I rather gather, particularly liked your country?' They would stick for the time to their English.

'It doesn't, I fear, seem particularly mine. And it doesn't in the least matter over there whether one likes it or not—that is to any one but one's self. But I didn't like it,' said Charlotte Stant.

'That's not encouraging then to me, is it?' the Prince went on.

'Do you mean because you're going?'

'Oh yes, of course we're going. I've wanted immensely to go.'

She waited. 'But now?—immediately?'

'In a month or two—it seems to be the new idea.' On which there was something in her face—as he imagined—that made him say: 'Didn't Maggie write to you?'

'Not of your going at once. But of course you must go. And of course you must stay'—Charlotte was easily clear—'as long as possible.'

'Is that what you did?' he laughed. 'You stayed as long as possible?'

'Well, it seemed to me so—but I hadn't "interests". You'll have them—on a great scale. It's the country for interests,' said Charlotte. 'If I had only had a few I doubtless wouldn't have left it.'

He waited an instant; they were still on their feet. 'Yours then are rather here?'

'Oh mine!'—the girl smiled. 'They take up little room, wherever they are.'

It determined in him, the way this came from her and what it somehow did for her—it determined in him a speech that would have seemed a few minutes before precarious and in questionable taste. The lead she had given him made the difference, and he felt it as really a lift on finding an honest and natural word rise, by its license, to his lips. Nothing surely could be, for both of them, more

in the note of a high bravery. 'I've been thinking it all the while so probable, you know, that you would have seen your way to marrying.'

She looked at him an instant, and during these seconds he feared for what he might have spoiled. 'To marrying whom?'

'Why some good kind clever rich American.'

Again his security hung in the balance—then she was, as he felt, admirable. 'I tried every one I came across. I did my best. I showed I had come, quite publicly, *for* that. Perhaps I showed it too much. At any rate it was no use. I had to recognise it. No one would have me.' Then she seemed to betray regret for his having to hear of her anything so disconcerting. She pitied his feeling about it; if he was disappointed she would cheer him up. 'Existence, you know, all the same, doesn't depend on that. I mean,' she smiled, 'on having caught a husband.'

'Oh—existence!' the Prince vaguely commented.

'You think I ought to argue for more than mere existence?' she asked. 'I don't see why *my* existence—even reduced as much as you like to being merely mine—should be so impossible. There are things of sorts I should be able to have—things I should be able to be. The position of a single woman to-day is very favourable, you know.'

'Favourable to what?'

'Why, just *to* existence—which may contain after all, in one way and another, so much. It may contain at the worst even affections; affections in fact quite particularly; fixed, that is, on one's friends. I'm extremely fond of Maggie for instance—I quite adore her. How could I adore her more if I were married to one of the people you speak of?'

The Prince gave a laugh. 'You might adore *him* more—!'

'Ah but it isn't, is it,' she asked, 'a question of that?'

'My dear friend,' he returned, 'it's always a question

of doing the best for one's self one can—without injury
to others.' He felt by this time that they were indeed on
an excellent basis; so he went on again as if to show
frankly his sense of its firmness. 'I venture therefore to
repeat my hope that you'll marry some capital fellow;
and also to repeat my belief that such a marriage will be
more favourable to you, as you call it, than even the spirit
of the age.'

She looked at him at first only for answer, and would
have appeared to take it with meekness hadn't she perhaps appeared a little more to take it with gaiety. 'Thank
you very much,' she simply said; but at that moment their
friend was with them again. It was undeniable that as she
came in Mrs Assingham looked with a certain smiling
sharpness from one of them to the other; the perception
of which was perhaps what led Charlotte, for reassurance,
to pass the question on. 'The Prince hopes so much I
shall still marry some good person.'

Whether it worked for Mrs Assingham or not the
Prince was himself, at this, more than ever reassured. He
was *safe*, in a word—that was what it all meant; and he
had required to be safe. He was really safe enough for
almost any joke. 'It's only,' he explained to their hostess,
'because of what Miss Stant has been telling me. Don't
we want to keep up her courage?' If the joke was broad
he hadn't at least begun it—not, that is, *as* a joke; which
was what his companion's address to their friend made
of it. 'She has been trying in America, she says, but
hasn't brought it off.'

The tone was somehow not what Mrs Assingham had
expected, but she made the best of it. 'Well then,' she
replied to the young man, 'if you take such an interest
you must bring it off.'

'And you must help, dear,' Charlotte said unper-
turbed—'as you've helped, so beautifully, in such things
before.' With which, before Mrs Assingham could meet
the appeal, she had addressed herself to the Prince on a

matter much nearer to him. '*Your* marriage is on Friday?—on Saturday?'

'Oh on Friday, no! For what do you take us? There's not a vulgar omen we're neglecting. On Saturday, please, at the Oratory, at three o'clock—before twelve assistants exactly.'

'Twelve including *me*?'

It struck him—he laughed. 'You'll make the thirteenth. It won't do!'

'Not,' said Charlotte, 'if you're going in for "omens". Should you like me stay away?'

'Dear no—we'll manage. We'll make the round number—we'll have in some old woman. They must keep them there for that, don't they?' Mrs Assingham's return had at last indicated for him his departure; he had possessed himself again of his hat and approached her to take leave. But he had another word for Charlotte. 'I dine tonight with Mr Verver. Have you any message?'

The girl seemed to wonder a little. 'For Mr Verver?'

'For Maggie—about her seeing you early. That, I know, is what she'll like.'

'Then I'll come early—thanks.'

'I dare say,' he went on, 'she'll send for you. I mean send a carriage.'

'Oh I don't require that, thanks. I can go, for a penny, can't I?' she asked of Mrs Assingham, 'in an omnibus.'

'Oh I say!' said the Prince while Mrs Assingham looked at her blandly.

'Yes, love—and I'll give you the penny. She shall *get* there,' the good lady added to their friend.

But Charlotte, as the latter took leave of her, thought of something else. 'There's a great favour, Prince, that I want to ask of you. I want, between this and Saturday, to make Maggie a marriage-present.'

'Oh I say!' the young man again soothingly exclaimed.

'Ah but I *must*,' she went on. 'It's really almost for